PURR~suasion

RENEE RIVA

Pink Heart Press

Copyright © 2018 Renee Riva

All rights reserved.

ISBN: 1986042278
ISBN-13:9781986042277

PURR~SUASION

To Cora~ whose kind heart reminds me of Zoey

&

To animal lovers everywhere~ for helping to protect and care for those sweet creatures who depend on us and enrich our lives~

Proverbs 12:10

"A righteous man regardeth the life of his beast..."

King James

Thank You, Jane Austen, for sharing your gift with the world.

The Setting of the Story

Leavenworth, Washington

With its beautiful Alpine mountains as a backdrop, Leavenworth, Washington was built to replicate a Bavarian village. It has become a favorite tourist destination for the December Christmas Tree Lighting Festival, following the ever-popular German Festival; Oktoberfest. Its charming chalet-style hotels and cafes give one the feel of being in a small village in the Bavarian Alps.

Chapter One

Standing on her deck above the Backstage Cafe, Zoey Pappas scanned the shops lining Leavenworth's main tourist thoroughfare, searching for any hint of a white, fluffy ball of fur. It wasn't until her gaze landed on the alleyway behind the small theatrical playhouse that she spotted her white Persian kitten schmoozing with a big tabby cat. Zoey turned and headed straight out the door of her studio chalet, down the back staircase, and crossed the street.

"Sofie!"

Sofie ignored her, apparently more interested in her new love interest.

"You little flirt." Zoey scooped her up and received a "r-e-e-r," in protest.

"You're grounded."

"I think she deserves another chance," a voice resounded from the open doorway to the playhouse.

Zoey narrowed her gaze on the shadowed entrance. A young man stepped into the daylight.

"That's my cat, Valentino, whom yours was 'flirting' with."

With sleek, dark hair and deep-set eyes, the young man behind the voice carried himself with an air of confidence that bordered on arrogance. Tall and broad-shouldered, he made her feel small, which at five-foot-eleven, seldom happened. A head taller than most girls her age, Zoey was used to standing out in a crowd. If her height wasn't enough, her jet-black hair and olive complexion drew even more attention. She knew the stately young man standing before her likely shared her same fate when it came to receiving public attention. Uncomfortable with standing out, working in her dog grooming shop with nothing but canines was a nice reprieve.

"My cat was only flirting because *your* cat obviously encouraged her to escape and cross the street," Zoey replied.

Dawson stooped to pet Valentino while Zoey continued to accuse him.

"He meows to her whenever she goes out on my deck. She is actually an indoor cat," she added.

Dawson smiled. "She looks like an outdoor cat right now."

Zoey blinked back at him. *Smart-aleck.* "Well, she's still pretty new in town and I'm afraid I'll lose her if she gets out on her own."

"You must be new in town, too." An extended hand and warm smile replaced his witty remarks. "I'm Dawson. Dawson Michael James."

Zoey reluctantly clasped his strong, warm hand, which engulfed hers. "I'm Zoey. Zoey Zeta Pappas."

Dawson stepped back. "Whoa. What kind of name is that?"

"A much more traditional name than someone whose name sounds like it's backwards."

"Backwards? What do mean, backwards?"

"I mean, it would sound more normal as James Michael Dawson."

Dawson smirked. "Oh, really? Well, where did yours come from? Did your folks name you after some movie star?"

Zoey flinched at his remark. "Excuse me? That's quite a comment coming from someone with a name that sounds straight off the set of *The Wild Wild West.* My name happens to be a very traditional Greek name in honor of Saint Zoe of Rome. But since nine out of ten people in America insist on pronouncing it as Zo, I added *y* to the end in grade school to avoid confusion for people like you."

Dawson laughed. "Is there a history lesson that goes with every Greek name, or just yours?"

Zoey shook her head. *Clueless.* "If you knew any Greek history or mythology, you would know that Zoe means life, and Zeta is the sixth letter in the Greek alphabet, and also means last born. Pappas means Priest. So, Da-w-w-w-son," Zoey drawled, "where did your name come from?"

"Well, Zoe-*y*, I obviously can't compete with yours. Not a lot of history involved in my name. *Dawson* was actually my mother's maiden name."

I knew it. Last name first.

"*Michael* was my paternal grandfather, and *James* is my

father's last name. No clue what the meanings behind any of them are in Greek or otherwise." Dawson narrowed his gaze. "How long have you been in town?"

"We moved from Seattle last month."

"We?"

"My cat and I."

~

Dawson tried to mask his relief in hearing "we" referred to a cat rather than a guy. He almost hated to admit how attracted he was to Zoey Zeta Pappas—presumably, along with every other guy who laid eyes on her. She really was gorgeous, even in jeans with holes in the knees. He felt flustered just looking at her. But, even more than her looks, he enjoyed her feisty spirit.

"What kind of plays do they perform here?" Zoey asked, peering at the old brick building.

"Mostly classics. Right now, they're holding auditions for Jane Austen's *Persuasion*."

Zoey lit up at the mention of Jane Austen. "Oh, I love *Persuasion!*" she exclaimed.

"Really?" Dawson looked surprised.

"Are you in the performance?"

"I am. I'm playing Captain Wentworth. They're still in search of my leading lady to play Anne Elliot." Dawson's heart raced at the thought of Zoey auditioning. Should he encourage her? He wanted to, but whoever played Anne needed to be quiet and meek, and not externally beautiful. Zoey commands attention. Maybe she could make herself less attractive.

~

Zoey stared at Dawson. "Are…. you…. okay?"

"Oh, uh, yeah." He realized he'd been staring at her. "I was just wondering…have you had any acting experience?"

Zoey winced. "Why do you ask?"

Dawson considered his words. "If you have, I wondered if you might be interested in auditioning for Anne? We aren't having much luck finding the right person for the part and rehearsals start next week."

"What? Me, act in *Persuasion?"* She laughed, nervously. "I haven't acted since …" Zoey fell silent.

"It's a fairly light role—I mean, it is the lead role, but your character—the character of Anne—is more observant than talkative. You wouldn't have as many lines as you might expect."

~

Zoey's furrowed brow was Dawson's first clue that he may have been too pushy in asking her to audition for the leading lady in a play. What was he thinking? That was the problem—he wasn't thinking—he was reacting to seeing someone he'd love to have as his leading lady, and he'd acted foolishly. He had to back pedal before she wrote him off as an overzealous idiot and walked away. "You know what? Rather than answer right now, how would you like to have a personal tour of the playhouse? Your cat is welcome to accompany you."

Dawson was relieved to see her shoulders relax.

"Why not?" She scooted Sofie onto her shoulder and followed Dawson and Valentino through the backstage door. "How long have you been involved in theater?"

"This playhouse has been in our family for twenty-five years," Dawson replied. "You could say we're a stage family. My folks are hoping to turn it over to me soon, but I have to decide between pursuing Broadway or running a small-town playhouse."

"That's quite a decision."

"You're telling me." Dawson ran a hand through his clean-cut hair and laughed. "I keep forgetting I just cut my hair short for this part. I haven't had it this short since my sister made me her beauty parlor victim as kids."

Zoey smiled at him. "It looks nice on you."

"Yeah?"

"Yeah. It kind of gives you the commanding air that

Captain Wentworth exudes."

"So, you really are familiar with the performance?"

"I know most of it by heart."

After seeing the props room, costume room, dressing rooms, stage, and auditorium, the tour came to an end. Dawson walked Zoey back to the alleyway door where they'd met. He couldn't resist the temptation to try again. "I hope you'll consider reading for the part."

"I appreciate the tour, but don't count on me auditioning," she replied.

Chapter Two

 Knowing Rocket, a hyperactive Labradoodle who viewed bath time as playtime, Zoey arrived at the grooming salon a few minutes early and suited up in her waterproof apron. She sprayed down her bathing tub to warm it up. Rocket was a rare case, one of the few dogs she didn't have to drag, push, or bribe to get into the wash tub.

 Seconds after the doorbell chimed, in pounced Rocket with all engines on *go*.

 "Okay, boy, let's get you clean!"

 Rocket leapt up the ramp and flew into the tub like a missile on a mission and slid to a halt. The minute Zoey turned the spray on, he began chomping at the water, delighted with the flying mist. Rocket spun and played while she lathered his coat, leaving Zoey and the walls covered in suds. She could hardly wait for the day when she could hire a full-time bather.

Three dogs later, Zoey put her *Out to Lunch* sign in the window, and headed to The Backstage Café. She loved being able to walk to work, home, and lunch, especially on the brink of spring with the scent of sweet apple blossoms in the air.

Zoey was greeted by Carla, a peppy twenty-something waitress who loved bright red lipstick. She popped a double bubble and welcomed Zoey. "*Guten Tag.* Want a booth and a burger?" she asked, smacking her gum.

"No, just the counter today, thanks. I have a client in thirty minutes."

"You got it!" Carla led her to the counter. "Our wiener schnitzel's on lunch special today."

"Actually, I'm going to be difficult and order a Cobb salad with Thousand Island on the side, and ice water with lemon, please."

"You got it!" she replied, and jotted something on her scratch pad.

Before Zoey had a chance to see who she was seated next to, a deep voice commanded her full attention.

"Looks like someone had fun during bath time today."

Zoey swerved to her right and stared straight into a pair of dark, shining eyes. "Oh, hello." She hadn't realized she was still soaking wet, or, that she had taken a seat right next to Dawson Michael James. "I had one dog who loved his bath, and three who hated theirs, so there's no way of escaping the drenched look."

"It looks good on you." Dawson smiled at her, then sunk his teeth into a giant German sausage dog.

"Good, huh?"

Dawson nodded and wiped his mouth. "Best sausage in town." He pierced Zoey with his glance. "So, have you decided to end my agony and audition for Anne Elliot?"

She sighed. "You know, I just don't feel compelled to add anything more to my life right now. By the time I've washed and groomed six or seven dogs, I'm usually ready for a pair of flannel pajamas and a good book."

"I have no problem with you rehearsing in your pajamas if you'll take the part."

Zoey smiled. *They must be really desperate to find an actress.* "So, who would I be auditioning against for the role?"

"Uh, well, it might be easier than you think. We don't have any Anne tryouts scheduled, so all they need to know is that you can memorize and deliver your lines, and look halfway decent in a long gown—which I'm certain you would."

"Who are 'they'?"

"They, as in, my mom and dad. My dad directs, and my mom covers the auditions."

Carla slid a salad bowl onto the counter and Zoey unrolled her fork from a paper napkin. She crunched away on crisp lettuce while she rolled the idea of acting around in her head.

"So, are you considering auditioning?"

She dabbed her lips with her napkin. "I'm thinking about it. Give me a few more days."

"You got it," he replied with a teasing smirk, repeating their waitress's favorite line. He gathered his wallet and jacket. "Back to work. I have an audition coming at one o'clock for the part of Anne's snobby sister. This gal should be a shoe-in for the part."

Zoey laughed. "That's kind of scary."

"You're telling me." Dawson smiled back, then headed for the door.

Zoey popped the last grape tomato into her mouth and waved Carla over. "I'd like my ticket now."

Carla blew out a giant bubble and sucked it back in with

a pop. Her bright red lips curved into a brilliant smile. "Already paid for."

"What? Who?"

Carla nodded toward the front window.

Zoey turned on the bar stool and saw Dawson with his hands shoved deep into his pockets crossing the street toward the theater. She watched him until he disappeared through the back door. How long had it been since anyone had paid for her meal? It seemed forever since a gentleman had treated her.

~

Returning home from work, Zoey dropped her purse in front of her apartment door with the crooked number three dangling by one nail. She made a mental note to buy Super Glue on her next trip to the store. Digging for her keys, she heard Sofie meowing from inside. "I'm coming," she replied, and jiggled the old lock with her key until it clicked open.

On her way through, Zoey scooped up Sofie and plopped her on the kitchen counter while she made herself a cup of tea. She glanced out her kitchen window to admire the newly opened tulips in her flower box, when Valentino leapt from a tree branch onto her railing. She slid open the glass door to intercept the uninvited intruder.

"Hey, buster, who invited you to drop by?" She picked up Valentino, despite his protest. "Sofie is much too young to be getting involved with a tomcat. You really need to go back where you came from." Zoey carried him through the apartment and headed back to the playhouse. "If you were looking for a little action, you aren't going to find it on my deck with my cat."

When the two of them arrived at the backstage door, Zoey knocked, but no one answered. She took the liberty of walking in. She found Dawson in the middle of a rehearsal with an actress he addressed as Lady Russell. Dawson was dressed in a captain's uniform looking quite dignified. His hair was combed back on the sides, and his tall stature and build exuded authority.

As soon as Dawson looked over and saw his cat with Zoey, he set down his script. "Is something wrong with Valentino?"

"Yes, Valentino has been living up to his stage name, rehearsing his Latin lover stunts. I caught him swinging from the alder tree onto my deck to pursue my cat—who is not yet spayed. I came to ask if you could find a way to keep him off my deck."

"That's the only reason you're here? I was kind of hoping you'd changed your mind about auditioning."

"Nope, sorry to say, I haven't. At this point I'm more concerned about having to deal with a litter of kittens."

Dawson gently pried his wayward cat from Zoey's arms and set him down with a quick scruff behind the ears. "I'll do my best to keep Valentino at street level, but there's no way I can know what he's up to every minute of the day." He glanced down at his purring cat. "I can hardly confine him when he's used to wandering around town and climbing trees. The fact is, he's not officially my cat. He's a stray who has adopted the theater, so I have very little authority when it comes to telling him where he can and cannot go."

Dawson placed his captain's hat back on his head. "If you're really concerned, you might consider having your cat spayed or keep her inside."

Zoey didn't like being told what to do with her cat, but somehow Dawson's boldness made him somewhat more appealing. Most men backed down when she got assertive, but not Dawson. He seemed to know his limits and where he wanted to draw the battle lines. He had just drawn some pretty strong lines with Zoey. As much as she hated to admit it, he was right about it being her responsibility to deal with her own cat.

"I'll see what I can do about getting an appointment at the veterinarian," she replied. "Does Valentino follow you to work every day?"

"Valentino goes wherever he feels like going, and The Backstage Theater seems to be his current home of choice—except at dinnertime. Then he crosses the street to the café and cons the waitresses out of the daily special, which is why he's teetering on the brink of obesity. He has all the gals over there tossing scraps to him right outside their kitchen door."

Dawson glanced at Lady Russell, waiting to resume their rehearsal. "I should get back to work." He tipped the brim of his hat, and started back, but suddenly stopped and glanced at Zoey. "By the way, would you like to see the gown that's been chosen for Anne?"

A gown? Costumes were her weakness. "I guess I could take a quick peek." Zoey gave Lady Russell an apologetic smile on her way to the costume room.

Dawson sifted through a dozen dresses before he came upon the one Anne would be wearing to the engagement dinner party in the last scene of the play. He pulled out a long elegant black gown with a gold bodice and gold threading throughout that shimmered, even in the low lighting.

"Oh, that is *fabulous*." Zoey couldn't help but reach out and touch the fabric. She slid her fingers over the shimmery satin and silk, so different from the cheap, faux costume material she was used to. Picturing herself in the gown beside the gallant sea captain, she had second thoughts about auditioning . "What does the rehearsal schedule require?"

Dawson's eyes brightened, as if he sensed her resolve weakening. "Four nights a week, evenings from seven to nine."

Zoey thought it over. She didn't have to work in the evenings, and nine wouldn't be terribly late as she only lived across the street. "I *might* reconsider," she commented, surprising herself as well as Dawson.

"That's great. I'll give you a copy of the script to look over while you decide."

Just then, a cute little blonde walked in the back door and looked sheepishly at Dawson. "Hi. Sorry I'm late."

Dawson shifted his gaze. "Amanda," he remarked.

Amanda shot Zoey a suspicious glare. Zoey knew by Dawson's expression that he'd caught the look too.

"Amanda, I'd like you to meet Zoey. She's considering playing the part of Anne."

Amanda moved closer to Dawson. "Oh, I thought Pamela was taking that part?"

"No, Pamela decided she had too much on her plate, so we really need to get somebody cast quickly." Dawson turned again toward Zoey. "Amanda is playing the part of Anne's older sister, Elizabeth."

That figures.

Chapter Three

Zoey fell asleep with two thoughts on her mind. First, acting alongside of Amanda would likely be very unpleasant as she obviously had something for Dawson and considered Zoey a threat to their happiness. Second, *that dress*, that absolutely gorgeous dress. She could not get it out of her mind.

Zoey left for work thinking about the gown. She thought about it again while washing Duke the Great Dane. Thought about it on her lunch break. And, she thought about it as she bathed and rinsed Molly the Saint Bernard.

It was still on her mind that evening when she plopped down on her deck, bare feet propped on the rail, sipping a warm cup of ginger tea. She stared across the street at The Backstage Theater. "What do you think Sofie, should I give this a go or am I completely crazy to even think about it?"

Her cat responded with a casual meow that Zoey interpreted as "Go ahead, maybe I'll get to see that cute tomcat again if you do."

While Zoey contemplated the idea, Dawson exited the back playhouse door and made his way across the street to The Backstage Café beneath her apartment. Before ducking inside, so not to appear that she was stalking him, Zoey did take a little extra time watching him stride across the street. She couldn't help notice how handsome he looked in his casual jeans and t-shirt. Perhaps she would just ask him a few questions about the part he was encouraging her to audition for.

"I'll be right back, Sofie. You hold down the fort while I'm gone. And no carousing!"

Zoey made her way down the back staircase and entered through the front door of the café, searching the room for a tall handsome actor. She spotted him right off sitting at a corner booth, alone. She crossed the dining room and approached his table.

"Hey," Dawson sounded surprised. "What are you up to?"

"I actually came in to talk to you."

"Really? Have a seat."

"You're not expecting anyone to join you?"

"Nope, just you."

"Why would you be expecting me?"

Dawson shrugged. "No reason, other than I saw you watching me from your deck."

Zoey scoffed. "I *wasn't* watching you."

"Yes, you were."

"No, I *wasn't*. You happened to be crossing the street at the same time I happened to be sitting on my deck."

Dawson laughed. "I'm just teasing you. Please, have a seat before you make a scene."

Zoey rolled her eyes, feigning exasperation, and slid into the booth across from him.

"Can I order you something to eat?"

Now that he'd mentioned it, she was rather hungry. "What are you having?"

"I haven't ordered yet, but how about sharing a pizza?"

"Sounds great."

"Are you vegan, vegetarian, lactose intolerant, or have any food allergies?" Dawson asked.

"None of the above."

"Thank goodness." He turned toward the waitress. "One large pizza combo, please."

"You got it!"

Both Dawson and Zoey looked at each other and grinned as the waitress headed toward the kitchen.

"So, Zo, what's up?" Dawson asked. "Is my cat harassing your cat again?"

"No, *Daw,* but he is responsible for why I'm here, being he was the reason we met."

Dawson cupped his chin in his hand and focused on Zoey with raised eyebrows.

"I'm here to ask a few questions about the play. I'm not saying I'll audition—I just have a few questions."

The corners of Dawson's mouth curved up and a glint appeared in his eyes. "Great. Ask away."

"Okay, you said rehearsals are from seven to nine, but specifically, what nights? Also, when is opening night, and how many performances do you offer?"

Dawson leaned back. "Rehearsals are Tuesday, Wednesday, and Thursday evenings. Saturday mornings are ten to noon. Opening night is eight weeks from our first rehearsal. We offer six performances—Friday and Saturday nights, and Sunday afternoon, so two weekends in a row."

Zoey took it all in and did some calculations in her head. "How many cast members are there?"

"A dozen total, but six main characters: Mr. Elliott, Anne, her sisters; Elizabeth and Mary, Captain Wentworth, and Lady Russell. Then another half dozen or so minor characters."

"Are all the main parts filled but Anne?"

"Yes. Just waiting on you…er…Anne." Dawson grinned.

Zoey couldn't help but blush when she noticed the way his dimples popped out when he grinned. They made him look like a school boy. She felt warm glancing at his adorable smile, and suddenly blurted, "I'll do it."

"You…you'll audition?"

Did I just say that? She stammered "I…I will. When should I come?"

"Tomorrow—whenever you get off work."

The pizza arrived enabling Zoey time to digest what she had just done. She was used to being in control. She didn't do anything she couldn't control and made sure she didn't have to rely on anyone but herself. She'd chosen where she wanted to live and how she wanted to support herself. She even controlled her breathing whenever she felt anxious. She took a few small breaths just to prove it. *What is this guy doing to me?*

"So, what brought you to Leavenworth?"

Not now. That was the one topic she did not want to visit. *It's okay. You've got this. Give him the short, edited version.*

Zoey dabbed pizza sauce from her lips while gathering back the reins. "After a disappointing career pursuit, I wanted to move away from the city—but I had no idea where, or how I could make a living. One night, on a whim, I got this harebrained idea to give my cat one of those lioness haircuts."

"Lioness cut?" He chuckled. "They have cat groomers now?"

"They do, but I thought I could do it myself."

A subtle smile emerged from Dawson.

"I got out a pair of old electric shears and attempted to shave her myself."

Dawson raised an eyebrow with increased curiosity. "She let you shave her?"

"No, but I insisted. By the time I was finished—or I should say, gave up—Sofie looked like she'd been in a back-alley brawl with a mean feral cat."

Dawson laughed. "Poor Sofie."

"Oh, it was awful. She had patches of hair missing from

her neck back to her tail, and big tufts of fur around her head. I was horrified and called around to find someone who could make her look somewhat normal again. There were very few cat groomers at the time. I finally found *Classy Cat Cuts* in Madison Park, who were experienced in exotic cuts for cats, and had many wealthy clients in the Madison Park and Broadmoor area. They were known for giving cats the lion do—for a ridiculous price."

"People can actually make a living in cat grooming?"

"If they're in the right place with a wealthy clientele. Long story, short, the groomer, Jill, made Sofie look adorable, like a little white lioness, and I was thrilled. Watching Jill in action triggered something in me and I knew what I wanted to do. I wanted to be a pet groomer."

"Seriously? Just like that?"

"Just like that. At that point in my life, I needed a break from people. Animals calm my anxieties. Anyway, I was able to take a grooming course from Jill and we became friends. I told her my dream of opening a grooming salon in a small town. She encouraged me to look into tourist towns. We both agreed that my business would have to be geared mostly toward dogs to make it anywhere other than Madison Park. Jill felt it would appeal to pet owners on vacation."

"How so?"

"Vacations tend to bring out the fun side of people." Zoey smiled. "You should see the look on their faces when the family returns to find their fur-kids looking like a lion or hyena."

Dawson raised his brow. "Hyena? How do you make a dog look like a hyena?"

"Have you never seen a baby hyena with a six-inch-high mohawk?"

At the shake of his head, she said "So adorable."

"The things we miss out on in small towns," Dawson mused.

"Not anymore," Zoey assured him.

~

Entering The Backstage Theater, Zoey showed up to audition with her script in hand. It was the first time she'd entered through the front door.

"You made it." Dawson sounded surprised that she'd actually followed through. She couldn't blame him. She'd hesitated all along and even thought about backing out at the last minute.

Dawson's parents came out to the lobby to meet her. She saw where Dawson got his looks. His mother, Claire, was a tall, natural beauty, and his father, Ben, was just an older version of his son.

"It's a pleasure to meet you both," Zoey responded, once introduced.

"Have you had any acting experience?" Ben asked.

"Some, yes."

"Have you chosen a scene you'd like to read for us?" Claire asked with a pleasant demeanor that helped ease Zoey's nerves.

"I have. I thought I'd read from the scene where Anne and Captain Wentworth are walking home. It's near the end, where they discover they have both loved each other all the time they've been apart."

"Oh, lovely," Claire replied. "My favorite scene." She glanced over at her son. "Dawson, I think you should step into your role as well to give the proper responses."

Dawson grabbed a script for himself and flipped toward the back. finding the page Zoey would be reading from.

"If you could begin here," she said, pointing to his line.

Dawson cleared his throat.

"To see you in the midst of those who could not be my well-wishers; to see your cousin close by you, conversing and smiling, and feel all the horrible eligibilities and proprieties of the match! To consider it was the certain wish of every being who could hope to influence you! Even if your own feelings were indifferent, to consider what powerful supports would be his! Was it not enough to make the fool of me which I appeared? How could I look on without agony?"

Dawson circled Zoey as he spoke, drawing closer with each accusation, piercing her heart by eyes filled with pain. She'd never been so moved by an actor before. Her hand nearly reached out to comfort him.

"Was it not the very sight of the friend who sat behind you, was not the recollection of what had been, the knowledge of her influence, the indelible, immoveable impression of what persuasion had once done—was it not all against me?"

Zoey replied as Anne. "You should have distinguished. You should not have suspected me now; the case is so different, and my age is so different. If I was wrong in yielding to persuasion once, remember that it was to persuasion exerted on the side of safety, not of risk. When I yielded, I thought it was to duty, but no duty could be called in aid here. In marrying a man indifferent to me, all risk would have been incurred, and all duty violated."

The way she looked at Dawson all but undid him as he struggled to continue with his dialogue. *Oh, to have a woman look at me that way one day!*

He gathered his wits and continued. "Perhaps I ought to have reasoned thus, but I could not. I could not derive benefit from the late knowledge I had acquired of your character. I could not bring it into play; it was overwhelmed, buried, lost in those earlier feelings which I had been smarting under year after year. I could think only of you as one who had yielded, who had been influenced by any one rather than by me. I saw you with the very person who had guided you in that year of misery. I had no reason to believe her of less authority now. The force of habit was to be added."

Zoey was no longer Zoey, she was Anne Elliott who looked longingly, lovingly into the eyes of the man she had been persuaded to turn down years ago, against every ounce of her own wishes and being. "I should have thought that my manner to yourself might have spared you much or all of this."

Dawson looked tormented. "No, no! Your manner might be only the ease which your engagement to another man would give. I left you in this belief; and yet, I was determined to see you again. My spirits rallied with the morning, and I felt that I had still a motive for remaining here."

The scene ended, but the chemistry did not. The air was

electrified, as though two lovers had spoken these very words to one another, with all of the emotions included. The room was so still you could hear the rustle of pages from the script. Dawson and Zoey forced their eyes away from one another and turned toward their directors.

Claire and Ben shared an embarrassing glance, then looked down at their shoes. Zoey's cheeks burned as Claire fanned her face with a copy of the script.

Ben cleared his throat. "Um, yes. That was quite, um, nice. Congratulations, Anne Elliott, you are our new leading lady."

Claire nodded in agreement. "Very well done, dear. I'd say you have had more experience than any of us anticipated. Welcome aboard."

Zoey backed nervously away from her leading man. "Th-thank you, all." She nodded to Dawson as well. "I'd better get back to let my cat out," she remarked, and walked swiftly toward the door.

~

Dawson smiled as he watched Zoey exit through the backstage door. *I thought you said your cat was an indoor cat?*

Chapter Four

"Zoey, dear, may I discuss something with you regarding your role as Anne?"

Zoey glanced up at Claire and laid the magazine aside. "Of course."

Claire took a seat at the vanity next to Zoey. "I feel a bit awkward bringing this up, but you are probably aware that Anne Elliot is not particularly beautiful—externally, that is. As the novel portrays, she was quite a beauty at the time she met the captain, but after eight years of facing spinsterhood, her beauty was … fading.

Zoey nodded, wondering where Claire was trying to go

with this.

Claire wrung her hands a few times which worried Zoey.

"I've never really had to approach anyone on this before, and I hope you will accept it as a compliment along with a dose of coaching. As you are naturally beautiful, even strikingly so, I'm wondering if we can downplay that a tad for the first few scenes by using an ivory foundation. You have such a natural olive complexion that I feel we may need to make you more pale, dear, and gradually work up to your natural skin color as you and Dawson—or, I mean, Captain Wentworth—fall deeper in love."

Zoey blushed at the mention of it.

"We can take some creative license in allowing Anne's beauty to increase the more time she spends around the captain and she begins to gain her glow again."

Zoey's mouth twitched against her willing it not to. "Uh, sure, if you feel that will better portray Anne, I'd be happy to do that." Zoey reached for the magazine. "I could find some less flattering, or simpler hair styles as well, and work into fancier styles as the play proceeds."

Claire breathed a sigh of relief. "Oh, thank you for understanding, dear. It's not often I have to ask someone to look less attractive than they are. I hope I haven't offended you."

"No offense taken," Zoey reassured her. *There could be worse things.*

"Well, good. I'm glad you are so easy to work with." She glanced toward Amanda, who was primping in the mirror at the vanity along the far wall. "Not everyone takes advice so easily," she added, quietly. "Wish me luck in explaining to Amanda that she can't dress like Cinderella for every scene."

Zoey smiled, appreciatively. "Good luck," she whispered. She gathered her things and decided it would be better if she wasn't present for the Cinderella conversation.

On her way down the back hall, Zoey nearly ran into Dawson as he exited the props room.

"Oh—sorry!" she exclaimed.

Dawson stopped and set down the rolled-up backdrop he was carrying. "Hard to see around these monstrosities."

Zoey eyed the canvas roll, then Dawson. "As long as you're here, may I ask you about something?"

"Sure, what's up?"

"I realize that Elizabeth's character is supposed to be a bit snarky, but would you know the reason for Amanda's snarkiness toward me, even after rehearsal is over?"

"Are you referring to those nasty glares Amanda's been giving you?"

"Exactly. I'm not sure if it's something I'm doing, or if it is my presence that bothers her."

Dawson glanced down the hall and lowered his voice just above a whisper. "Unfortunately, there's a little bit of history where Amanda and I are concerned. She played Scarlett O'Hara in the last play, and I was Rhett Butler. I hate to say it, but I'm afraid I may still be Rhett in Amanda's mind." He twisted his lips in a wry smile. "Along with the fact that she did try out for the role of Anne Elliott before you came along and didn't make the part. So, I would say there's a little fuel for animosity toward you. None of your doing."

"You're saying I not only got the part she wanted, but I'm leading lady to Amanda's Rhett Butler— in this case, Captain Wentworth?"

"Exactly. I really haven't done anything that I know of to encourage her in that vein, other than acting my part as well as I could, which may have confused her."

Zoey smiled. "I have a feeling that happens in Hollywood too. I always wondered how those actors and actresses can be in those intense love scenes together and be completely detached—even though there are cameras and lights surrounding them. Still, if I were kissing Clark Gable in *Gone with the Wind*, I'm not sure how much of that passion would have been acting."

"Clark Gable? Really? What is it with women and Clark Gable?"

"Do you really have to ask?" Zoey laughed. "Besides the obvious, he would have done anything for the woman he loved. I think we've lost the chivalrous heroes in present day drama."

"Yeah, I hate to admit it, but I think you're right. Things are pretty watered down these days."

Zoey tipped her head to the side. "Is that why you went back to producing all the classics?"

"That's a pretty observant deduction on your part. That's exactly why I like the classics. I prefer scripts where right wins over wrong, good wins over evil, and somehow, love wins out in the end. I guess I'm more of a black and white kind of guy."

"I'm not real fond of gray myself," Zoey replied.

"Well, Miss Elliott, I'd say we have a few things in common, on and off stage. Now, may I ask you a few personal questions?"

"You can try," she replied.

"First, where did you get your acting experience, and, second, why did you stop pursuing it?"

Zoey released a long sigh. "I attended acting classes at

Northwest Theater Company in Seattle, and, was halfway into the course when I realized I no longer cared to pursue acting."

"I *knew* you'd had professional training. No one just walks into an audition and performs the way you did."

And no one but me knows I wasn't just acting.

"So, what happened?" Dawson asked.

How do I explain that I was sick of being looked at as an object rather than an actress? "Well, I enjoyed improving my acting ability, but I did not enjoy living among the theatrical community off-stage. Too much...."

"Drama?"

"Yes. Everyone was so .... "

"Theatrical?"

Zoey smiled. "Yeah. Go figure."

Dawson nodded.

"*And*, the productions they had us working on were nothing like I'd hoped for or expected. I was playing characters I couldn't relate to, nor wanted to relate to. When my director insisted I play the part of a 'sexy, cynical, female vampire', something in me snapped. I wanted to run away to a quiet place in the country with no more vampires or crowds, no more playing weird characters or taking on bizarre assignments. We weren't performing any of the old classics—just new material that didn't sit well with me. I went home one night and told my cat we were moving."

"And that's when she got her back-alley-brawl haircut that led to Puppy Dooz."

Zoey nodded. "And here I am back on stage—but a far cry from the one I left."

"I'm glad you gave it another shot. You really are a remarkable actress, Zoey."

Zoey looked down to try and hide her flushed face in the hallway shadows. "Thank you," she said, softly. "I poured a lot into my acting career. It's nice to feel appreciated for my ability rather than…." She looked away, not finishing.

Dawson laid his hand gently on her arm. "You are appreciated here, Zoey. More than you probably realize."

Before Zoey could respond, he hoisted the canvas roll onto his shoulder and headed down the hall.

Chapter Five

The small Greek Orthodox Church was tiny compared to the church she'd attended in Seattle. She loved the stillness and peace that surrounded her as she lit candles for those she loved and missed, both back in Seattle, and those who had passed on, especially her grandmother. Sitting alone reminded her of her large Greek family who used to accompany her to church every Sunday. She glanced around at the other families sitting together and felt sad for being apart from her family for the first time. Still, she felt close to them just being in the church. It comforted her to know that those she missed were still connected in heart and spirit.

By the time Zoey left the sanctuary, she felt uplifted. Rather than return home, she'd planned ahead to stop and take a hike along Icicle Ridge. At the trailhead, she changed into a pair of hiking shorts and boots, then headed up a trail that overlooked the Wenatchee and Icicle Rivers. With orchards in full bloom, the air was fragrant, and the sunshine felt warm against her skin as she crested the hill.

Looking back at the hillside she'd just climbed, she noticed a figure coming up the trail toward her. At first glance, she thought it was Dawson, but, chided herself, sure it was just wishful thinking.

"Hey, Zoey! Is that you up there?"

Of all places, how did the two of them end up on the same trail?

"Dawson Michael James, are you stalking me, or what?" She yelled back.

At the point he met up with her, he did have a small confession to make. "I was driving back from Wenatchee and couldn't miss your bright green car at the trailhead as I passed. I couldn't resist joining you for a hike. I hope you don't mind. I was happy to find somebody I know out hiking on such a great day. "

"Well, then, I hope you packed us a lunch because I just realized I am starving up here."

Dawson swung a small pack around from his shoulders. "I always stop at fruit stands when I'm in Wenatchee. You want an apple, a nectarine, or a peach?"

"One of each." She laughed. "I still can't believe you're here."

"Hey, check out this view." Dawson led Zoey to the edge of the cliff. Sitting along the canyon ridge, the two gazed down at the sun-sparkled rivers below.

After two juicy peaches and a nectarine, Dawson broke the silence. "So, what are you doing way out here?"

"I just went to church in Wenatchee. It's the closest Orthodox church I could find."

"Orthodox? How did you find Orthodoxy in America?"

Zoey smiled. "When you're Greek, you don't find Orthodoxy, you *are* Orthodox. The same way Italians in Rome are Roman Catholic. I am Orthodox because my father was Orthodox, because his father was

Orthodox, because the whole country of Greece was Orthodox. Whereas, in America there are over thirty thousand Christian denominations—you all seem to like choices for everything in this country."

"We are definitely in the *Land of Opportunity*."

Zoey turned toward Dawson with a quizzical glance. "What is your faith, Dawson?"

"I'm .... searching." He had a far-off look. "Have you ever questioned your beliefs?" he asked.

"Of course."

"What have you questioned, if you don't mind me asking?"

Zoey thought. "I remember as a child, looking at icons of the saints who'd lived for God. I wondered why they all looked so sad. If faith brings peace and joy, why are they not smiling and looking prettier? So, one day, I took the icons from the wall in my bedroom and decided I would make them look prettier and happier." She smiled at the memory. "With paints and brushes, I made their hallowed cheeks rosier. I even tried to cover up the bags under the eyes of St. John the Baptist."

Dawson grinned. "You did not."

"When my mother discovered what I'd done, she

took me to church to talk to my priest. He explained how every stroke that goes into painting the icons has a reason behind it. 'If John the Baptist has bags under his eyes, there is good reason for it.' Then he said that most saints are not smiling because they were martyred for their faith in Christ. 'So you see, they would not be smiling then, but you can be quite certain, they are smiling now. 'Those who weep now shall laugh in the kingdom of heaven.'"

Dawson nodded slowly. "It must have been nice to grow up so confident of what you believe."

"It's comforting to feel a part of something so old and unchanged. It's not so much about what I want to believe or a philosophy." Her eyes pierced Dawson. "It's about love. God loving us and us loving in return. Regardless of the differences, we're all connected to each other, you know?"

Dawson stared back and cocked his head to one side. "Are you sure you aren't really a nun in disguise?"

"If I were a nun, I probably wouldn't be complaining that I'm still hungry after three pieces of fruit and obsessing right now over where my next meal is going to come from."

"I know a great place to eat close by with the most incredible shrimp burgers."

"Let's go!"

Zoey made it down the mountainside in record time. "I'm following you!" she yelled, hopping into her car.

~

The bright green Hyundai pulled into the parking lot of *The Riverbend Restaurant* behind Dawson's pickup truck. Dawson led the way through a rustic cedar lodge nestled along the bank of the Wenatchee River. A large deck overlooked the rapids below. As soon as Zoey saw the river from the front windows, she requested outdoor seating. The waitress escorted them to a riverside table partially shaded by fragrant pines.

Zoey took a seat on the sunny side of the table and offered Dawson the shade. "After living on the westside all my life, I crave sunlight." It was barely noon so the heat wasn't too intense, especially with the gentle breeze that came off of the river. She turned her face to the sun, closed her eyes, and smiled. "I just thrive in sunlight."

"I've noticed that west-siders always eat outside over

here. They don't care how hot or cold it is as long as the sun is out."

"That's because we're all vitamin D deficient from three-hundred days of rain a year."

"Can I get you two something to drink?" the waitress asked.

Dawson looked at Zoey.

"I'll have iced tea with lemon, and he's ordering for me."

"Lemonade, please, and two Riverbend Shrimp Burgers with garlic fries."

"Sounds like you've been here before," the waitress replied, and scooped up the menus she'd just set down. "I'll get those started for you and be right back with your drinks."

"I love that smell." Zoey sighed. "We only smell pine like this at Christmastime where I come from." She glanced over at Dawson. "You aren't seriously considering giving all of this up for New York City, are you?"

Dawson shrugged. "I guess when you've lived in one place all your life you tend to take it for granted. I love it here, but sometimes I wouldn't mind something new just for the sake of change and new experiences." He gave her a reassuring smile. "Nothing definite yet, though."

"I'm glad I didn't have to go all the way to Hollywood to realize that the acting industry wasn't for me. They saved me a trip by bringing Hollywood to Seattle."

"I would think New York would be completely different from Hollywood. The stage and the screen are two different worlds."

The waitress delivered the drinks and disappeared back inside.

"There are differences, I'm sure, but there are similarities too. Where there's acting, there are a lot of egos involved." Zoey sipped her iced tea, then added, "I think it's easy to get swept away with the lure of the stage. From appearances, it can look like the ultimate life; being paid to perform at an art you love. But, once you get to see what really goes on behind the scenes, it's not quite as alluring."

"You mentioned you didn't care for all the drama, but what caused you to give it up completely?"

Zoey pushed her bangs out of her eyes after a strong gust of wind rearranged them. "A few years ago, some friends and I were hanging out after work at our favorite restaurant when all of these Paramount trucks started rolling in to the hotel next door. We went out to see what it was all about. Hollywood was coming to Seattle to shoot a movie. We started talking with one of the directors and let him know we were theater students. The next day, they approached us about being extras in their production. They usually had all the extras they needed when shooting in Hollywood, but since this was in a new location, they had to look to the community for help. My girlfriends and I were so excited, we jumped right in. Over the course of the two-week shoot, we did a lot of standing around.

"It's amazing how many takes they had to do for a five-minute scene. They spent an entire day on just one or two scenes. In all of our down time between takes, I was able to observe a lot behind the scenes. A number of the guys – from the ones working the cameras, to some of the actors themselves—spent a lot of time hitting on the pretty extras."

"I'm guessing you were included in their pursuits?"

"Fortunately, I made friends with the son of one of the producers who shared with me his dismay in the movie industry. He was pretty fed up with all the games he saw being played and how vulnerable all the young girls were to the attention from cast and crew members."

"Did you actually see it happening around you?"

Zoey nodded. "I saw a lot. I saw young girls leave the set with crew members or actors and return with them the next morning. Many of these men wore wedding rings and were a good deal older than the girls. When I was having lunch with the crew, one of the guys kept trying to talk me into going out after they wrapped it up that day. 'No strings attached,' was his selling line."

"That's deep," Dawson joked.

"Y-eah." Zoey sighed. "One of the extras I'd seen him leave with the night before saw him talking to me and came over. He didn't see her standing behind him. At the point she heard him asking me out, she started sobbing, 'What are you doing with her? I thought you loved me?'

"It was really sad, and I became very disenchanted with the whole thing. When we were almost done shooting, one of the directors called me aside and tried to persuade me to consider coming to Hollywood. By then I had seen enough to know better. No amount of money was worth what was going on there. I guess what I'm trying to say, is: you may think it's all about sharing your gift of acting and being appreciated or loved for it, but in the end, you find, it's not really love at all. It can leave one quite empty."

"Is that what happened to you? Is that why you quit and moved away?"

Zoey shivered, despite the warmth.

"What is it?" Dawson whispered.

Zoey looked down at her napkin and folded the corner

back and forth. "It was disappointing to find out the one thing I'd poured my heart into wasn't going to be received or appreciated the way I'd hoped."

Dawson nodded.

"I thought it would be different in acting school." Zoey shook her head, slowly. "My teacher was more interested in what I was doing after class than my acting ability in class." She glanced up at Dawson. The pain was evident as she choked out words. "I was *so sick* of being looked at *that way.*"

Dawson swallowed hard and looked away.

"When I refused going out with him, he completely ignored me in class and offered me no more help with my acting, even though he was my teacher."

Anger flashed in Dawson's eyes, but turned quickly to tenderness when he gazed back at Zoey. "I hope you feel differently working at our playhouse. You are definitely appreciated for your talent."

Zoey's eyes teared up. "Thank you, Dawson. Finding The Backstage Theater has been a Godsend for me. I hope you realize that too, without having to leave. It's a pretty vicious industry out there."

"You don't think I'd be strong enough to stand my ground?"

"I'm saying it would be very difficult when everyone around you is climbing the same ladder for their own gain, regardless of who they step on. I now consider peace of mind worth whatever I have to give up. God has a way of replacing what we think we've lost with something much more valuable."

"And what has He replaced your love of the arts with?"

Zoey smiled. *"Persuasion."* She glanced out over the river. "I've also changed my definition of 'The Arts.' Living out here in the mountains, I see the arts everywhere. Not art, as in something I created, but what He created. I find peace just breathing the air out here."

Chapter Six

On her way to rehearsal, Zoey caught a glimpse of Valentino milling around the dumpster. He suddenly pounced on something scurrying past him. Zoey made a beeline to rescue whatever unfortunate victim had fallen prey. By the time she cornered Valentino in the back alley, he had a small furry rodent in his clutches.

"Valentino, release him at once!" she scolded. The tomcat looked at Zoey as though she were crazy and dug his claws in even deeper. He seized the poor thing in his jaws and attempted a daring escape.

"Oh, no you don't, Buster." Zoey reached out and grabbed the cat, causing him to release his victim along with a loud "r-e-e-e-r". The furry gray critter tumbled from his mouth and remained frozen in place.

After shutting Valentino inside the backstage door, she returned to his startled victim. She kneeled closer. "You poor little thing, you must be in shock." She realized she was talking to a small gray rat. He didn't look terribly wounded but was definitely shook up by the whole ordeal. Zoey peered around and spotted a small cardboard box. She tipped it on its side and coaxed the little guy inside with a gentle nudge from her shoe.

Just as she got him secured in the box, the back door opened and a disgruntled Valentino shot out with Dawson on his heels. "What in the world ....?"

Zoey clamped the lid shut and stood up. She suddenly felt awkward explaining that she'd rescued a dumpster rat from a cat in a back alley. Not everyone understood people with rat compassion, and she wasn't ready to explain it just yet.

"Your cat was in pursuit of my new pet."

Dawson's eyebrows arched. "Your new pet?"

"Yes ... Sir Galahad somehow got loose and Valentino found him. Anyway, I'll just return him to my apartment and be right back for rehearsal."

"O-kay. Mind if I ask what kind of pet Sir Galahad is?"

"He's a... Silver Back Appalachian Rattus."

"Rattus? That sounds closely related to a rat."

"It's the scientific name, fancier than a common rat. I'd show him to you but he's rather shook up right now. Anyway, I'd better run him home—be right back!" She hurried on her way to leave her newly wounded rat at home with her cat. *This is getting complicated.*

Zoey returned to rehearsal, having left Sir Galahad locked in the bathroom with a capful of water and a small chunk of cheddar in his box. She'd added soft Kleenex and washed her hands well.

"I take it Sir Galahad is safe and sound back at the palace?" Dawson's lips twitched, as though he were holding back a smile.

"Safe and sound," Zoey repeated. She couldn't believe she had just fabricated an entire fairytale about a silly rat rescue. She knew her conscience would nag at her until she told Dawson the truth, but for now, the *Gallant Rescue of Sir Galahad* would have to suffice. She was becoming increasingly fond of Captain Wentworth and was hesitant to risk losing him over a germy dumpster rat. Certain men may not be able to handle the truth that a young lady as refined as Anne Elliott held a secret fetish for rats.

~

The play scene that evening took place at the dinner table of the Musgroves where Anne dined quietly while the two Musgrove sisters, Louisa and Harriette, vied for Captain Wentworth's attention. Anne and Captain Wentworth were to steal hidden glances from one another.

Unbeknownst to Zoey, a change in casting had taken place since the previous rehearsal. Amanda was now cast as Louisa Musgrove rather than Elizabeth, Anne's older sister. Not only was the cast change a sudden shock, but so was the color of Amanda's hair. Having died it from blonde to black for the part of Elizabeth, she'd now attempted to die it back to blonde with a high lift bleach. The effect was unavoidably distracting, as she now had three different shades of color, mostly orange, all crying out for an intensive conditioning treatment. Anne nearly missed her line trying to take it all in.

Not only had Amanda backed out from playing her original character, but she completely overacted the scene of Louisa trying to win Captain's Wentworth's attention. Amanda's performance went beyond anything that would have been considered prudent in the early 1800's. She fluttered her eyes and flaunted herself all over Captain Wentworth to the point they had to yell "cut" in the middle of the scene and give her instructions to tone it down.

It took Zoey a few more weeks of rehearsals to finally catch on to what Amanda was up to and her true motives for changing characters. First, Elizabeth only had lines early in the story, and not again until the end. Louisa, however, was Captain's Wentworth's main pursuer throughout the rest of the play. It all became clear the day they rehearsed the walk on the pier, where Louisa jumped from a high seawall into Captain Wentworth's arms. He was supposed to miss the second time she attempted the jump. Unfortunately, Dawson missed the first time, and Amanda crumpled into a pile on the stage floor. She threw such a fit that rehearsal was cut short that day.

Accepting an invitation to coffee following rehearsal, Dawson admitted to Zoey that he felt Amanda's true motives for the cast change were due to wanting more scenes with him. He also admitted that the look Amanda had in her eyes when Louisa leapt for his waiting arms, was so unsettling, it caused him to flinch when he went to catch her. "I feel awful that she landed on the floor, but it was like a flying cupid coming straight at me with an arrow."

"Why does your family feel such an obligation to accommodate her in your productions?" Zoey questioned.

"Guess who our largest sponsors are for keeping the playhouse open?"

"Her parents."

"Bingo. It's not so much that we're being bribed to accommodate her—she really is a good actress. I don't think my parents are aware of the extent of her attraction toward me, ever since playing Scarlett O'Hara in *Gone with The Wind*, when her acting ability looked promising."

"You must have played a convincing Rhett Butler."

"To my chagrin." Dawson smiled, and took a large gulp of coffee.

"When Louisa realizes that she's not going to win the captain's heart at the end of the play will she insist on taking my character?"

"I think she knows better. It only worked for Louisa because my former Louisa had to drop out of the performance so Amanda snatched it up, leaving the part of Elizabeth to fill instead. She didn't act this way until you came on board. She's always hung around the stage and been in a number of productions but never acted so possessive—until now."

"Well, that's ridiculous. Doesn't she know the difference between a play and reality? It's crazy for her to think just because the character of Captain Wentworth is in love with Anne that you'd be in love with me."

Dawson shook his head. "Yeah, pretty crazy." *Or not.*

Chapter Seven

Business at Puppy Dooz was keeping Zoey up to her elbows in suds. After a few canines were seen strutting around town as jungle lions and bear cubs, people began flocking to her salon to get their pets booked as soon as possible. Cindy Shelden was ecstatic when her black and white Pomeranian came out resembling a baby panda bear. Zoey could hardly get her door open in the mornings before people crowded into her waiting room, including one lady requesting pink hair for her French Poodle—as long as it was natural and hypoallergenic.

Fortunately, life on the stage seemed to settle into a nice flow, without too much more drama from Amanda, who was relishing her role as the doting admirer of Captain Wentworth. All went well until the captain and Anne had a scene where they declared their long-overdue affections for each other.

When Captain Wentworth went to help Anne into the carriage after a long walk, Louisa stole Mary Elliot's lines. "Why should Anne get to ride back? I'm clearly more tired than she is." She actually pushed Zoey away when Dawson went to help her into the carriage.

"What are you doing?" Dawson exclaimed. "You have no such lines."

Amanda quickly regained her composure. "Woops, I accidently recited Mary's lines." She apologized to Dawson, but not to Zoey, whom she'd nearly knocked over.

~

As the cast worked its way through the play night after night, and the Elliot family reunited in Bath, things began to heat up on and off the set. The scene where Anne and Captain Harville compared the loyalty between a man and a woman in love, while

Captain Wentworth listened nearby, Zoey felt increasingly closer to Dawson as her character, Anne, drew closer to Captain Wentworth.

When Anne declared, "As long as the one you love lives, there is hope. A woman loves longest even when it seems there is no hope," the look she received from Dawson penetrated her very soul. For the first time in her stage experience, she could not draw a distinction between acting and her true feelings. When she read aloud the love letter Captain Wentworth wrote to Anne, Zoey felt as though she were reading a letter written to her from Dawson. *Was this what happened to Amanda in* Gone with the Wind? *Does Dawson have this effect on every leading lady he acts with? Is it that he's such a great actor, or am I'm making a fool of myself the same as Amanda?*

After the final scene where the captain showed up to ask for Anne's hand in marriage, Zoey went straight to the dressing room and changed from the black and gold evening gown into her blue jeans and sweatshirt. She ran into Dawson on her way out.

"That was some amazing acting tonight," he complimented.

It was so amazing, she feared her flushed face

would give her away. "Gotta feed my cat!" she exclaimed, and hurried out the back door.

~

As opening night drew near, Zoey's enthusiasm for going to rehearsals began to override her zeal for going to work. It wasn't that her joy for work had decreased, but that her anticipation of going to play rehearsal increased. Dramatically. There were powerful dynamics going on behind the scenes of *Persuasion* that Zoey had little control over. Chemistry in particular. It seemed the longer Anne and Captain Wentworth were forced to remain apart, while their hearts yearned silently for one another, Zoey's emotions followed suit in her feelings toward Dawson. She was all for method acting and remaining in character apart from rehearsals, but this was beyond that technique.

By the time the cast had mastered all of their lines and were only a week out from opening night, emotions and chemistry between the captain and Anne Elliot continued to intensify. Zoey hoped she was the only one who noticed, but apparently the instincts of mothers surpass the odds when it comes to their sons. After the final dress rehearsal, Claire approached Zoey in the dressing room.

"You gave a wonderful performance tonight, dear." She smiled kindly at Zoey. "I must say, you certainly bring out the best in my son … my son's acting," she corrected. "It's nice to see him happy again."

"Oh, uh, thank you." *I think. What does she mean 'again'? Must be family skeletons—not sure I want to know more.*

Opening Night

A dimly lit stage revealed silhouettes of a full-house. Tickets sold out early in the week. The house lights came up as the opening scene of *Persuasion* came into view. Zoey, playing the subdued, twenty-seven-year-old spinster-in-the-making, showed little emotion, as she was instructed for the first few scenes, which mostly focused on the odd family dynamics. The once well-to-do family had lost their matriarch, and with that loss, went all prudence of spending by the indulgent father. They were now being told they would have to retrench in Bath and lease their home out to the admiral and his wife to help cover their financial expenditures.

Eight years prior, Anne, against her heart's desire, had been persuaded by Lady Russell, to refuse the proposal of marriage to Captain Wentworth due to his inferior income at the time.

When Captain Wentworth entered the room where his long-lost love stood across from him, the emotion between the two was palpable to the entire audience and remained so, growing in intensity with every scene.

The scenes that included Louisa, played by Amanda, threw even more fuel into the burning embers of love and jealousy. Glances exchanged between the handsome captain and Anne added flames to the fire as Anne grew more beautiful with each scene.

When Anne Elliot entered the stage in the final scene, she was so drop-dead gorgeous in her gold and ebony gown, the cast could hear audible sighs from the audience. Moreover, when Captain Wentworth arrived to ask Anne's father for his daughter's hand in marriage, Dawson actually faltered the minute he caught sight of Anne and had to regain his composure before delivering his lines. That sincere reaction made the scene even more poignant.

When Captain Wentworth finally bent down to give Anne the kiss he'd waited eight long years for, there was the sense that the audience was intruding on a scene far more intimate than a mere kiss, for they'd followed the agony of his unrequited love that lurked behind that long-anticipated kiss. The audience was left breathless.

~

The next four performances came off equally as powerful as the first, if not more so. It seemed each performance of *Persuasion* grew more intense between the two leading characters, to the point where people were talking about it and writing about it. Somewhere in the gossip pool, word made it to the ears of a well-known play critic who happened to be visiting family in the area. Little did Zoey know, following her closing night performance, a play review was rolling off the Wenatchee Valley newspaper presses while she celebrated with cast members in the reception hall of *The Bavarian Inn.*

The Eastside Review of Persuasion
Closing Night Performance

"On a lovely summer's eve in June, theatergoers filled the charming Bavarian-style playhouse that has brought joy to the quaint town of Leavenworth, Washington, for over two decades. The family-owned theater not only directs its own plays, but family members act in the performances as well. Little did any of the actors or directors realize, but in this sold-out audience of 150, one of its guests was none other than Zane Bellante, New York's well-known stage producer, best known for his hit play on Broadway, *Knights of Serena*. Bellante happened to be visiting family in Leavenworth and opted to take in a local play. His review of the performance was beyond all expectations and was quoted as saying, 'I have seldom experienced anything so delightful, so ignited with genuine talent and chemistry between lead actors, in particular, that of Captain Frederick Wentworth, played by Dawson Michael James, and his leading lady, Anne Elliott, played by Zoey Zeta Pappas.' He added that he hopes to work with these two rising talents in New York one day."

~

Dawson approached Zoey at the cast party in the Bavarian Inn reception hall and asked if she would like to duck out and have dinner with him downstairs. The Bavarian Inn had one of the nicest restaurants in Eastern Washington. Zoey felt a twinge of excitement as the intensity of their closing kiss still lingered on her lips. "I'm still in my gown," she replied.

"It's not a problem—I'm still in my naval uniform."

She agreed to go, but had to remind herself she was going to dinner with Dawson, not Captain Wentworth. His uniform didn't help matters.

The candle-lit dining room of The Bavarian Inn was grand and elegant. Zoey excused herself to the ladies' room while Dawson waited for the hostess to seat them. She checked herself quickly in the mirror, worried she might have lipstick on her teeth, or that her gown might be tucked into her Spanx in back. With a side glance in the mirror she was reassured all was well. She gave a quick twirl, enjoying the gorgeous gown for the last time. If only Austen-era fashions could have stayed forever.

Dawson stood when Zoey returned and the two were led to a table by the fireplace. Even though the days in early June were warm and sunny, evenings were still a little chilly. Dawson pulled the chair out for her nearest the fire, then took a seat across from her. He looked over and sighed. "That gold satin in the firelight really sets your eyes aglow."

Zoey smiled. "That's quite a line—is that a Rhett Butler line?"

"No, that's actually not a line. I just came up with that on my own when I looked at you."

"Oh." Zoey blushed. "It sounded so poetic, I thought, perhaps it was from a classic."

"Nope, just classic Dawson."

The waitress returned with two glasses and a bottle of sparkling cider.

"Bubbles …?" She looked at Dawson inquisitively. "Are we celebrating something?"

Dawson uncorked the bottle himself and began to pour. "As a matter of fact, there is something I wanted to celebrate with you."

Zoey's heart beat faster. She hoped he was going to

confess that he couldn't separate his feelings from those of Captain Wentworth's for Anne, any more than she could separate her feelings from Anne for the captain.

"Zoey, I hope you know how much I've enjoyed acting with you and getting to know you. I've seriously *never* met anyone like you."

That's not hard to believe. Rat lover and all.

"Which is why I want to share this moment with you…"

Breathe.

"Zoey, I'm going to New York."

Zoey's heart stopped. "You…you're what?"

"I've just received notification from the Manhattan Academy of Dramatic Arts—the one I'd applied for and had little hope of getting into—and they've accepted me!"

"That's…that's wonderful." Her eyes filled with tears. "I'm so happy for you." Tears rolled down her cheeks.

"Zoey…are you okay?" He reached for her hand and covered it with his.

"I'm …fine, really. I'm…happy for you. And I'm going to miss you." She grabbed her napkin and pressed it to her eyes. "I'm sorry—I was just really surprised."

"Aww, Zo, please don't cry. I didn't realize…."

"That you'd be the one leaving, and I'd be the one missing you?"

"I didn't realize you cared this much. I mean, I've always cared for you—I just didn't know it was reciprocated—but, I'm really glad it is, which makes it even harder for me to leave."

"No, Dawson, you must go. This is an amazing opportunity for you. You have a chance of making it to Broadway now, and that's your dream. This isn't the time to be worrying about relationships. Besides, if it doesn't pan out in New York, I'll probably still be here washing dogs and rescuing alley rats until I die…"

"Rescuing alley rats?"

"Oh, well, yeah, but that doesn't matter right now."

"Wait…yes it does. I don't want to miss this—what's this about rescuing alley rats?"

Leave it to me to bring up rats at a time like this. "Oh, it's just that I lied to you about Sir Galahad—he was really just a mangy little street rat I rescued from your cat. I was worried you'd think I was too weird if I told you the truth, so now you know, and it doesn't matter anymore since you're leaving…"

"You're wrong. It does matter." Dawson pulled his chair over by the fire right next to Zoey. He turned to face her. "It matters, because that girl who cares about wounded alley rats is the girl I have fallen in love with."

A tingling warmth encircled her heart. "You ... you love me?"

"That shouldn't surprise you. I just haven't said anything because I've known all along I'd be leaving at some point and it wouldn't be fair to you. Besides that, I seriously doubted you felt the same for me."

"You really thought I was acting all this time?"

"You weren't?"

"Why do you think we had such great reviews?"

Dawson grinned. "I wasn't acting either." He glanced around the nearly empty restaurant, and whispered, "You think anyone would mind if we rehearsed that closing scene one more time?"

"Who cares?" Zoey whispered back, and kissed Dawson as the girl who hadn't yet kissed the man she loved—the man she may not kiss again for a very long time.

Chapter Eight

Zoey did her best to keep her mind on work and off of Dawson. Still, she checked her mail daily—sometimes twice. Nearly three weeks passed before she heard from him for the first time.

Dear Zoey,

There has been so much to take in since I've arrived, I've hardly had a chance to put my thoughts into words. I have never experienced anything like this before. The first few weeks in New York City were mesmerizing; the lights and the energy of the city in comparison to Leavenworth, it's electrifying. I feel as though a part of me I never knew existed before is coming alive. Or maybe I have sensed it there but it has taken a place like this to really bring it out.

I am never at a loss for things to do here. I walk the streets, go to shows, eat at unbelievable restaurants and cafes. I even went to a theater on Broadway where I hope to be auditioning someday. Sitting in the audience, watching was amazing. Something inside of me woke up and came alive for the first time—taking it all in; the dimmed lighting, the energy of the actors when they came out on stage.

My classes start this coming week, for which I am more than ready. I have an orientation tonight to meet all of my instructors and acting coaches. I'll try to write again once things are rolling and I feel I have a grasp of things here. For now, just know my spirit is soaring and I wanted to be able to share my thoughts with you. I hope things are going well for you and your puppy cuts, your cat, and Sir Galahad. Give my best to Valentino if you see him hanging around The Backstage.

All my best,

Love,

Dawson

Zoey released the letter and let it flutter to the ground.

"*If* I see Valentino," she repeated. *You mean when I see your poor cat, sitting outside The Backstage, crying and waiting for you day and night. He's no longer even interested in pursuing Sofie.*

Zoey sank into her reading chair and stared straight ahead. Sofie leapt into her lap and curled up. "Well, ol' girl, it looks like it's just you, me, and Sir Galahad from here on out. Sounds like our captain fell for the Big Apple."

Sofie purred contentedly. Sir Galahad was busy running his tenth mile of the day on his big new Rat-Runner wheel. Zoey hung her head and cried.

Give it time, her heart softly reminded her. *You've been there yourself before.*

"But that was me," she whispered back.

Zoey's only recourse was to keep her peace, enjoy her animals, stay busy, and pray. Whenever she felt prone to depression or let her thoughts wander, she tried to draw on her favorite prayer written by one of the Orthodox Church fathers:

"Lord, give me the strength to greet the coming day in peace. Help me in all things to rely on Your holy will. Reveal Your will to me every hour of the day. Bless my dealings with all people. Teach me to treat all people who

come to me throughout the day with peace of soul and with firm conviction that Your will governs all. In all my deeds and words guide my thoughts and feelings. In unexpected events, let me not forget that all are sent by you.

Teach me to act firmly and wisely, without embittering and embarrassing others. Give me the physical strength to bear the labors of this day. Direct my will, teach me to pray, pray in me. Amen."

~

One month later....

Dear Zoey,

I went to my first audition a few days ago for a part in a small local theater. It's for the Shakespearean play Much Ado About Nothing. *It was for the role of Claudio. I felt I did the best job I had ever done in auditioning for anything before. Then came the waiting. I knew I would drive myself crazy if I didn't keep occupied so I rode buses, I took taxis, I walked miles, and took in a movie.*

I got my call back. I made the cut. I was so stunned I sat there and stared out the window and thought, I'm in. I'm finally part of this crazy New York lifestyle. This is my new home. This is where I will live out my dreams. New York City.

I took myself out on the town and had a meal that I'll never forget, then spent a fortune and took in a Broadway show, envisioning myself as one of the actors. I was walking home about midnight; the city was still alive and I thought, Wow, what a contrast to Leavenworth! The whole town would be sound asleep by now and getting up shortly for those who have farms and animals to care for.

I sat in this tiny little rustic studio apartment that I pay a fortune to lease, and suddenly, something hit me. Something in the depth of my being just knew this is where I belong. Maybe this is something that everyone feels when they become a part of a true community they've longed for. For some, it may be a small town like Leavenworth, for others a bustling, thriving city like New York. Maybe I'll wake up tomorrow and I'll feel differently but, for now, I'm enjoying being part of something I've only dreamt about before. I guess time will tell.

By the way, did I mention that Amanda showed up here? I just about fainted the first time I ran into her. She is doing surprisingly well. New York seems to be in her blood as well and is bringing out a side of her I'd never seen before. She's quite amazing on stage. She's already getting parts in some pretty big productions. I'm actually quite proud of her. I think she finally found her niche in life. It's funny that we both ended up here.

Well, that was a lot to convey all at once. I hope all is going well for you, Sofie, and Sir Galahad. I will be pretty swamped between classes and performances so not sure when I'll have a chance to write again. Give my best to my family. I'm hoping they'll come to my opening night but it's

still a long way off. Thanks for listening to me ramble.
With fond memories,
Captain Wentworth

~

Fond memories? That's it? Isn't Claudio the young soldier who falls in love with Leonardo's beautiful daughter? Perfect.

It was the last letter Zoey received. She didn't know what to think, other than he was saying goodbye. He didn't even mention her coming to visit with his family for opening night. Will Dawson's new leading lady fall for him the same way she and Amanda did? Did he come to realize that he and Amanda had a lot in common after all? It would drive Zoey crazy to try and guess what Dawson was thinking or doing. *Lord, help me to keep this day in peace...*

~

In contrast to a long, hot summer, winters in Leavenworth were cold and snowy. The extra activity and bright lights of the Christmas Tree Lighting festivities helped keep customers coming through the doors of Puppy Dooz. The extra services and joy revolving around The

Nativity season at church helped keep Zoey's spirits up. She only had time to think about Dawson when she walked by the playhouse on her way to work and back. Or when she looked out her window and the playhouse stared back. Or when she ate at The Backstage Cafe and glanced over at the corner booth where she and Dawson always sat.

Zoey mailed Dawson a Christmas card with some friendly news about the latest happenings around town, but never received one in return. Her highlight of the holidays was having her family come visit for Christmas. Zoey's little studio was wall to wall family, sleeping bags, and presents. All was well until her mother asked, "So, honey, is there a special man in your life from your side of the mountains?"

Zoey wasn't even sure how to answer that. There was a special man in her life, but Zoey was no longer in *his* life. "Not at the moment," was the best she could come up with.

As winter thawed slowly into spring, Zoey's hope of ever hearing from Dawson melted along with the winter snow.

~

Zoey was just cleaning up after a long Monday afternoon when the Puppy Dooz bell sounded. She found

Claire Dawson in her reception area. She knew that Claire and Ben had left town the previous week and assumed they had gone to New York to see Dawson's performance of *Much Ado About Nothing.* Claire was a painful reminder that Zoey was not included, but the look of concern on Claire's face halted Zoey's thoughts.

"Claire, is something wrong?"

Claire tried to look cheerful. "No, dear, I just wanted to stop in and see how you were doing. It's been so long since we've seen you at the theater."

"Oh, well, I'm up to my ears in dogs, but business is good." *Why are you really here? Is Dawson engaged?*

"We've just returned from New York." She tried to sound cheerful, but it wasn't working.

"Yes, I assumed you probably went to see Dawson's performance on opening night."

"Yes, yes, it was … it was excellent."

Zoey couldn't stand the waiting. "So, how is Dawson?"

Claire glanced around nervously. "Honey, am I disrupting your work right now—is there a better time…"

"No, I'm just tidying up." Zoey came around the counter to the reception area and motioned for Claire to take a seat in the large Victorian chair, while Zoey sat in the adjacent velvet chair. "Please, tell me the news from afar," Zoey prompted, bracing herself.

Claire's cheerful facade fell away, replaced by tearful eyes of a concerned mother. "Oh, Zoey, I just don't know what to do. It's Dawson." She sighed heavily. "His father and I had always hoped he might one day want to take on our little theater and keep it going. It's the only legacy we have to offer our children and future grandchildren. But we also want our children to choose their own path in life. As you know, Dawson's sister chose to move for the sake of her husband's work, which we completely understand and support."

So Dawson is marrying someone and staying in New York and there's no one to carry on the legacy.

Claire reached over and took hold of Zoey's hand. "I don't think you knew this, but before you came to Leavenworth, Dawson was going through a terrible depression. He'd just lost his best friend in a car accident they were in. Dawson survived, but his friend, Thomas, didn't."

Zoey was shocked. Dawson had never said a word about it.

"He shut down for a time and we weren't sure how to help him. He lost hope, and his faith in God. He didn't feel he deserved to still be here when his friend couldn't be.

But, I want you to know, dear, after you came to town, our son came alive again. He came back to us. When we saw him rehearse with you for the audition, we had hope again for the first time."

Zoey clasped Claire's hand tighter. Her own eyes teared up. "I had no idea."

"His father and I hoped that Dawson might stay and rebuild his life here, but we didn't want to hinder him from pursuing his dream of Broadway either. It's just that, when we saw him in New York, even though he says he's happy, and his future as an actor looks bright, we noticed that he no longer has that glow that he had whenever we saw him with you."

A tear fell from Zoey's eye.

"I don't want to burden you with this, but I sensed that perhaps you were sad he left as well—a mother can sense things like this. I'm worried he's hurt you, and I'm sorry, too."

"It's not your fault. It sounds like he has a lot of pain to work through."

Claire nodded. "I came to ask a favor of you."

"What is it?" Zoey asked.

"Would you pray for my son?"

Zoey blinked back more tears. "Yes, yes, of course I

will."

"I don't know God's plan for him. I did not sense that Dawson was interested in anyone in New York. He asked about you. When I began to talk about you, I saw a flicker of the old Dawson again. I don't know what it is that is holding him there, but I think it's just something he needs to work out on his own." Claire looked at Zoey with hopeful eyes. "Am I right in feeling that you still care about my son?"

"Yes," Zoey whispered. "Very much."

Claire looked pleadingly into Zoey's eyes.

"Please don't give up on him."

"I won't," Zoey replied, softly. "Thank you for letting me know."

"Thank you for loving my son."

After Claire left, Zoey turned off her OPEN sign and went for a long walk.

Chapter Nine

Zoey usually stood for most of the church service, but today, she felt heavy and weighed down. She found a seat along the back wall and sat down. She let the words and music wash over her like a soothing balm to her aching heart. It would take time to heal this time. She had never been in love before. And especially, an unrequited love. She didn't realize anything could be so painful with no visible, gaping wound to show for it.

Following communion, she closed her eyes and prayed for God's comfort. She sensed others walking past her to their seats during the closing prayers. She felt someone brush by her and take the seat next to her. She slowly opened her eyes and glanced over.

Dawson.

"Hey," he whispered, tenderly.

Zoey blinked, wondering if it was actually Dawson. "What are you doing here?" she whispered, still not believing it was really him.

"Your foolish captain has returned from the sea."

During the closing hymn, Zoey wavered between hurt, anger, and love, and wasn't sure which of the emotions was stronger at the moment. "Have you come for a visit?"

He shook his head.

"You've come *back?*" she whispered, glad that people were filing out, paying no attention to them. Questions crowded her mind. *What about school? What about Shakespeare? What about Claudio's leading lady? Or Amanda?* Now the anger was winning out.

He shook his head. "No." He looked reverently around the church, then turned back and, glanced into Zoey's eyes. "Not back," he replied. "I've come *home.* I hope it's not too late."

~

There were moments when Zoey's heart soared that Dawson had finally seen the light. There were other moments where she thought of all the time she'd been left hanging to wonder if she'd ever see him again. And, there were moments when she was determined that it was too late—too late for her heart to ever recapture what she once felt just before Dawson announced he was leaving for New York. She tried not to force or hinder any feelings for Dawson but kept busy and figured her heart would land wherever and whenever it decided to land.

Zoey could tell Dawson respected her apparent coolness toward him, and knew it was for good reason. He tried not to persuade her one way or the other, besides *coincidently* showing up at the grocery store when she did her shopping, or arriving at The Backstage Café directly after her. He also stopped by Puppy Dooz with his cat, insisting that Valentino really wanted a flea dip and lion-mane haircut. By the time Zoey finally peeled Valentino down from the drapes attempting to escape, she was convinced otherwise. Zoey did have to admit that Dawson's efforts to engage her were getting more creative and somewhat entertaining.

One morning, when Zoey had just finished clipping Finnegan, a shaggy sheepdog, his owner, Sandy, returned. She and Zoey had become good friends due to Finnegan's weekly shampoos. Sandy's neighbor owned a community trout pond that Finnegan loved to sneak into. He constantly smelled like fish, hence, the weekly shampoos. Sandy eyed Zoey with a funny look on her face.

"What? Did I do something wrong with Finnegan's cut?"

"No! I just have an unusual favor to ask."

Zoey braced herself. "What is it?"

"My daughter, Kyra loved you in the play *Persuasion* and was captivated by your character and beautiful gown. Her eighth birthday party is Sunday afternoon and I was wondering if, by any chance, you could just come by in that gorgeous gown and wish her a happy birthday. She's going to have a dress-up tea party with three other little friends so it would be a surprise for them all."

Zoey blinked a few times. She'd never had a request like this before. "Umm….well…."

Sandy looked at her pleadingly. "I know it's a lot to ask, but you have no idea how much it will mean to my daughter and her friends. They look up to you as someone they'd like to emulate, and I love giving them positive role models at their age. It's not often I can introduce my daughter to someone who is beautiful and gifted and loves animals and God. I just want her to know such people are real and live right here in our town."

"Wow. I can hardly say no to that." Zoey laughed, taken

aback by all the compliments.

"Oh, good. Then you'll do it?"

"I will. As long as I get to have a piece of birthday cake while I'm there."

"As much as you want!" Sandy gave Zoey a quick hug. "Oh, I'm so happy. You've no idea how much this means to me." She grabbed her dog, gave Zoey a gigantic tip, and left the shop, all smiles.

~

Sunday afternoon, Zoey stopped by the theater on her way to fulfill her tea party obligation. She tried to be quiet, as the dress rehearsal for *Little Women* was in full swing. Dawson's folks had begged her to try out, but her heart just wasn't into it. As she sifted through the costumes, Dawson appeared at the door. "I thought I heard someone in here."

Zoey had just located the gown. "Oh! I didn't realize you were here. I was going to ask your mom if I could borrow Anne's engagement dress, but I'll just ask you."

"Are you getting engaged?" he joked.

Zoey laughed. "Hardly. I've been asked to attend a little girl's tea party for Sandy's eight-year-old daughter and friends. They were somewhat taken by Anne Elliot, according to Sandy."

"They weren't the only ones," Dawson said, under his

breath.

"What was that?" Zoey asked.

"Oh, nothing. I was just saying, I'm not surprised."

"So, do you mind if I borrow the costume?"

"No, not at all. Did you want to use the dressing room and stage make up to recreate Anne?"

"That would be great. I don't really have time to run home and it would be much easier to leave from here." Zoey whisked the gown off the rack, then headed for the dressing room. "Thanks!" she called over her shoulder.

Dawson hung around nearby in the props room and was watching when Zoey reappeared in full costume and make up. His heart lurched the minute he saw her. The sight of her in that beautiful gown brought back all of the emotion he'd felt for her on their closing night. The night before he left town and ruined all chances of ever being her Captain Wentworth.

Zoey caught the wave of emotion that passed between them, but tried to dismiss it. "I just realized something," she commented.

"What's that?" he asked.

"I may be hard pressed to fit this billowing gown into the driver's seat of my little Hyundai coupe."

Dawson smiled. "Have no fear, Miss Elliot, it would be

my pleasure to deliver you to tea in my classy Ford pick-up truck."

"That would be wonderful," she replied. "I didn't even think about it until I had this contraption on." She followed Dawson to the parking lot.

"You sure you don't mind giving me a ride home as well?"

"I'll be happy to." Dawson helped Zoey into the passenger side of the truck with the same line he gave her when he helped her into the horse carriage in the play. It did not go unnoticed by Zoey, as evidenced by the flutter in her heart.

"How long did you intend to stay?" he asked.

"Hopefully, just long enough for a spot of tea and a slice of birthday cake. Perhaps an hour?"

It didn't take long to arrive at Sandy's house as it was only a few miles from the theater. "I shall return promptly in one hour," Dawson announced, His hand lingered a moment longer than necessary while helping her down from the truck.

Zoey didn't try to pull away until he released her. Their gazes caught briefly before she turned away. "Thank you," she said, quietly.

Dawson nodded, then turned to go.

Zoey was greeted enthusiastically by squeals and giggles. She was swept inside by four little princesses dressed every bit as fancy as she was. Between the games, gifts, tea, and birthday cake, the time passed quickly by.

Zoey was taken by surprise when the doorbell rang an hour later. "That must be my ride," she announced.

"Awww," little Kyra moaned. "Can't you stay for the slumber party?"

Zoey laughed. "I wish I could, but, unfortunately, my horse and buggy are waiting to whisk me off back to the palace." As an afterthought, Zoey added, "If you'd all like to see the man who played Captain Wentworth, he's at the door waiting to take me home."

The girls scurried like excited mice and pulled open the front door. There, before their eyes stood the very dashing Captain Wentworth in full costume, including his big, fancy Captain's hat.

"What are you doing?" Zoey exclaimed.
"Why should you get all the glory?" Dawson replied, good naturedly.

Four little girls giggled and blushed at the same time.

Dawson lowered his brows in a pretend frown. "What's so funny? Haven't you ever seen a sea captain before?"

"Not on dry land!" Kyra exclaimed.

The girls all laughed.

"Would you like to stay for some cake?"

"I don't think my Captain trousers will fit if I do." He turned toward Zoey. "Well, Anne, are you ready to start off?"

"Sure." Zoey wished Kyra happy birthday again and gave all the girls goodbye hugs.

"Have fun with Captain Wentworth," they all teased.

Sandy saw them to the door. "I can't thank you enough. You made my little girl's birthday so special." She handed an envelope to Zoey. "Just a little appreciation gift—not a big deal—but I want you to know how grateful I am." Zoey opened the envelope and found a gift card for Bavarian Coffee Roasters—the best coffee in town.

"That is so sweet of you—and so unnecessary—but, thank you!" She hugged Sandy goodbye.

Once they stepped outside into the warm sunshine, Zoey glanced out to the street. "Where's your truck?"

Dawson glanced back. "I walked."

"You what?"

"It's so nice out, I thought it would be fun to walk you home."

"Do you realize it's over two miles—wearing costumes?"

"I do. It seemed to me that it was that long walk home in *Persuasion* where the captain and Anne were finally able to discuss everything that had gone wrong in the past, and everything they wanted to change for the future." Dawson turned to Zoey with the most sincere expression. "Zoey, it took eight years for the captain to finally reclaim the love he had lost with Anne. I realize eight months was a long time for me to disappear..."

"You didn't just disappear, Dawson. You left me hanging… with nothing to hang onto. You declared your love for me before you left, then, the next thing I get is a letter telling me you've found everything you've ever wanted in New York City. After that… nothing."

Dawson began walking, sorting out his thoughts. "New York was transforming… in many ways. I had never been anywhere like it. I admit, I got completely swept up in having a desperately needed distraction from my real issues."

Zoey listened, keeping stride with Dawson's leisurely pace.

"But, when you're running from something, over time, you realize, you can't outrun yourself. So, there I was – different surroundings—same issues." Dawson stopped and stared into Zoey's eyes. "There's something I need to tell you. Before you came to town, I lost a close friend. He was like a brother." Dawson choked up. "Part of my leaving was trying to get away from that memory. All the distractions in New York kept my pain at bay. But, once the noise died down, I finally had to come to terms with my sorrow. It took me a while."

Zoey just nodded.

"His death affected more than just my relationship with you. It affected my trust in God as well. I turned my back on Him for a time. After thinking over all you'd said about your faith, and how it grounds you, I realized I wanted to know that God was still waiting for me. I needed a solid anchor—unchanging.

"I actually found an Orthodox church in Manhattan and began meeting with the priest. One of the first things he told me was, 'The church is like a sturdy boat already afloat. Rather than struggle in the water alone, or build your own raft, you just need to get into the boat.'

"I stopped trying to find a church that fit my individual preferences, but realized, what I needed has always been there—I just needed to become part of what already *Is*. The priest told me to just 'Stay in the boat.' That's the only way I've been able to stay afloat."

Zoey smiled at Dawson.

"I never did stop thinking of you."

"It might have been nice to have heard that once in a while," Zoey replied, candidly.

Dawson looked down at his hands. "I know. I didn't think it was fair to involve you when I didn't know what my future held. If I told you I still loved you, it would give you reason to hold on, but if I decided to stay in New York, which I sometimes thought I might, it would only hurt you more. Either way, I hurt you. I know that—especially now. I was hoping that maybe you'd just forget about me and move on."

"I tried to. It didn't work."

Dawson smiled. "I'm glad it didn't. I confess, I was worried that you'd have a number of admirers trying to win your heart."

"Well, there has been one, and I have to admit I'm rather fond of him, too."

Dawson's smile faded. "Oh. Is he still in your life?"

"He is. I've tried to set him free a number of times, but, he kept coming back, so I decided to keep him."

Dawson swallowed hard. "If you don't mind my asking, is it someone I know?"

"It is. He has beady little eyes, whiskers, and a long tail."

A grin replaced Dawson's look of despair. "Sir Galahad? That is some pretty tough competition."

Zoey laughed. Along with a twinge of guilt, there was a slight sense of satisfaction in making Dawson sweat a little, and to see that he cared.

"I really did try to set Sir Galahad free but he found his way back to my deck. I was worried the cats would get him, so I built him a nice big maze with tunnels and a main living space. He seems content to stay." Zoey glanced over at Dawson. "So, what about Amanda? I take it you two spent time together in some of the productions?"

Now, Dawson laughed. "Zoey, Amanda handled New York like she truly was meant to be there. She really found her place in the theater. She had no problem getting work. I'm happy to report that as soon as Amanda landed the lead role of Queen Elizabeth, she fell hard and fast for Sir Walter Raleigh and I was suddenly of no interest to her any longer. Anyway, we remained friends, and she's never had second thoughts of leaving Manhattan. Amanda will have to be the one to carry the torch and represent our small town of Leavenworth in New York City."

"That's pretty amazing," Zoey replied. "I'm really happy for her."

Dawson smiled. "Me too. I've also come to realize how

much my family and our theater mean to me and to the community of Leavenworth. I'd really like to stay and carry on our family tradition." He grinned. "Someone needs to keep a tradition going."

"I think that's a great start."

"But first, I need to make things right with those I've hurt." Dawson stopped beneath a shaded tree. He took Zoey's hands gently in his and looked into her deep brown eyes, Zoey, I am so sorry—I can't tell you how sorry … can you please forgive me?"

Zoey's eyes welled up. "I want to …" she began. "I want to trust you. I'd like to try again."

Dawson wiped a tear from her cheek, then wrapped his arms around her in a warm, loving embrace. "That day in church that I told you I had come home, I meant I'd really come *home*—to you, to my family, and, most importantly, to God. I finally understand it's not about the masses loving me. It's about me learning to love. I'm praying you will all give me another chance."

Zoey sighed. "If Anne Elliot can do it after eight years of waiting, I should be able to at least try." Then she pulled back slightly. "But, I warn you, Captain, next time your ship sails, you'd better make sure I'm on board with you."

"I promise, Zoey, no matter where I go from here, you

will be my first mate."

Zoey tilted her head up to her tall captain. "You may kiss me now to seal the deal."

Dawson pulled Zoey back into his arms and kissed her like a sailor who'd been away at sea far too long.

The End

The True Stories Behind This Story

Sometimes it's fun to hear where the inspiration and ideas come from that go into a fictional story. In many cases, fiction stories are not completely fiction. I wanted to share a few of the real-life stories included in *PURR~suasion.*

Along the lines of acting and Hollywood, my friends and I were working at a restaurant when the Paramount movie trucks rolled into town—just the way I explained it this story.

When I was twenty-years-old, I had the chance to become a "movie extra" in five Hollywood movies. An "extra" is hired as one of those anonymous faces in the background; people who walk down the street during a scene in a movie, or sit in a restaurant where the main characters are eating.

That summer, Hollywood shot a bunch of movies in Seattle. I put my name on a casting list, so when Hollywood came anywhere near Seattle, I was called up and given the part of playing an extra for $40 a day. My short-lived Hollywood career includes:

An Innocent Love: I was an extra watching a UW Crew race on the University of Washington campus, starring Melissa Sue Anderson who played Mary Ingalls in *Little House on the Prairie.*

The Jackie Kennedy Story: I was dressed up in 1960's style dress with a bouffant hairdo, and strolled through an airport with an old suitcase. Jaclyn Smith played Jackie. She's shorter than she looks in Charlie's Angels.

An Officer and A Gentleman: I watched an air show in a stand of bleachers at Fort Worden on Puget Sound. The airshow wasn't really happening but we had to look up and clap as though it was. They added that later, but then cut the whole scene. I walked right past Richard Gere between scenes—I am talking inches here—and realized he has a really big nose in real life. But he truly was a gentleman and thanked us all for helping with the movie.

Hot Pursuit: I played a mechanic on a conveyor belt at a candy factory in a cute white jumpsuit. This was a pilot for a series that never took off. Another day they shot a scene down on the Seattle waterfront and a stunt driver knocked her front tooth out on the steering wheel when she spun out in a chase scene by the ferry dock.

Murder She Wrote: I played a student in a college

classroom at the University of Washington, starring Angela Lansbury, who was not happy that we were still shooting the same scene at 11pm, so they called it a wrap. I played frisbee with Angela Lansbury's son between takes and sat by Peter Graves at lunch and talked about my Italian grandmother.

I had enough experience with Hollywood to know that it is the last place I would want to live and the last industry I would want to pursue, especially as a young lady. I got to see enough behind the scenes to know that it is not a female friendly place to work. I saw a lot of heartbroken young girls playing extras who were star-struck by the actors and crew members, and taken advantage of.

One day on the set, a director called me over and had me sit in one of his director chairs and asked if I had ever considered moving to Hollywood to get into acting or movies. He told me that it was a pretty incredible way to make a good living, and that I might want to pursue it. After seeing the way many of the actors and crew behaved, I no longer had any interest in pursuing that dream.

I continued to enjoy plays, and being in small productions, but I no longer took acting classes after that.

If you're wondering where Zoey's fetish for rescuing rats comes from, it can probably be traced back to my childhood as a hopeless animal lover. My neighbor, and best friend, Dorie, had a whole wooden milk box filled with little pet white mice that seemed to multiply each week. We spent hours making mazes for them and playing with them out in her garage. Because my own mother was not fond of rodents, I was not allowed to have pet mice, so a mouse rescue was my only option.

I rescued a mouse from Charlie, the neighbor's cat, and was allowed to let him recover in my Tarzan lunch pail, provided he lived up in my treehouse. I still haven't gotten over his tragic ending. My little brother snuck up in the tree house when I wasn't home and brought my mouse down to show my grandmother—because we all know how fond 80-year-old grandmothers are of mice—and he leapt out of the lunch pail and ran off the end of our deck that hung out over a very high cliff. My mother tried to tell me she saw him land softly on a leaf below, but I have my doubts.

That incident only helped me justify my next plan

of action. If it didn't bother my mother for me to keep a mouse somewhere that she didn't have to see it, then it shouldn't bother her for me to have a hamster hiding in my closet. At age ten, I rode my stingray bicycle to the pet store and bought a pure white hamster with beautiful red eyes, then rode home with her on my bike. I also bought a cage and hid Abigale the hamster inside the cage inside my bedroom closet.

I could hardly wait to get home after school each day and play with my little secret rodent up in my closet. I spent hours in there. Being that we had five children in the family, my mom didn't really notice when one of us went missing as long as we were home and at the table on time for dinner.

It only took three weeks for my mom to smell out the rodent. Poor Abigale ran away shortly after that and was never found. I'm hoping she had a wonderful life playing free in our woods.

I had to come up with a new plan. A few weeks before my birthday, I asked my mom if it was rude to give back a birthday gift. She said "yes." So, I asked my best friend to give me a hamster for my birthday, which she did. It drove my mother to tears, and I felt terribly guilty. But not guilty enough to give the hamster back. Not surprising, when I went to check the mail one day, there was an application for a girl's boarding school back East.

The scenario of the "embellished" icons is embarrassingly true. I've always been a bit of a challenge for priests. There was the time I told my mom I needed to talk to the priest because I was pretty sure I was "possessed" after watching previews of *The Exorcist*. I also used those cute little weekly offering envelopes with angelic illustrations, to write letters to God, asking him for a horse—minus my weekly offering.

On Forgiveness Sunday, our deacon asked me if I'd be coming back that night—when the church gathers before Lent to ask forgiveness from one another for our offenses throughout the year. I told him, "I don't think I've had the chance to have offended anyone yet," to which he replied, "You might be surprised."

When I grew up, I married a guy who was warned ahead of time that my lifelong dream was to have a farm, swarming with animals. After working and saving our dimes for ten years, we finally bought a five acre, red and white farmhouse with white fences and a matching barn, potting house, well house and dog house, in a Norman Rockwell setting. Within a very short time, we had horses, cows, pigs, chickens, turkeys, ducks, dogs, cats, bunnies, parakeets, parrots, hamsters, and fish.

One day, I came home with a pet rat that I couldn't resist because he only cost a dollar. My husband promptly told me that when you live on a farm you don't have to pay for rats. I found a nice home for him with a young girl from church who loved him until the day he died curled up in his food dish. What a way to go!

As far as the pet grooming incident, one very hot summer's day, I had the bright idea of helping my dog and cat stay cool. I bought a pair of electric shears and tried to give them summer haircuts. They both came out looking like they'd been in a back-alley brawl with tufts of fur missing here and there and no real rhyme or reason to the style. My dream of becoming a professional pet groomer was short-lived, but I did get to live out the dream through Zoey with her Puppy Dooz Salon.

And, now you know the true stories behind this story!

I hope you've enjoyed it!

If you enjoyed PURR~suasion, you might also enjoy the first chapter of *Jackson's Treasure*...

Chapter One
New Orleans, Louisiana 1905

Peyton Abercrombie slipped from the festive Piggot Manor Ballroom unnoticed in search of the ladies' room. Her curiosity coaxed her into meandering through the four-story mansion that was soon to become her home. Tonight, her stepfather, Archibald Abercrombie would announce her betrothal to Lord Pennington Piggot. Within weeks, she would become the mistress of the Piggot Plantation, one of the largest sugar plantations in New Orleans. The thought of marrying the snobbish Lord Piggot, twice her age and three times her size, was enough to halt the tour and lock herself into the third-story powder room. The candlelit mirror reflected her nausea.

"I can't go through with this."

Peyton glanced out the window that overlooked a moonlit bay. A large vessel caught her eye. Its huge sails ruffled in the breeze, beckoning her to escape and come aboard. Not one to turn down an opportunity, she swung her pantaloon-clad legs out of the third-story window and climbed down the rose trellis in her ball gown. Dropping to the ground with a thud, Peyton hoisted her gown above her knees and hurried down to the sandy cove, praying no one would see her.

The anchored schooner rocked gently in the protected bay. Peyton glanced around in hopes of spotting a dinghy along the shore. A short distance down the beach she found just the thing—a small rowboat pulled up onto the sand. Peyton stashed her silk slippers in the reticule tied at her waist, shoved the boat into the tide, and waded knee deep in her gown. She gathered her wet hem and heaved herself over the side of the dinghy, landing in the hull of the wooden boat. Locking the oars into place, Peyton was soon on her way to what she hoped would be an adventurous escape from a life of drudgery with a man she didn't love.

~

Jackson Lafitte devoured his bowl of beef stew by candlelight. As Captain of the *Mon Cherisse*, he was often the last to eat and the last to turn in for the night. He'd already sent his crew to their berths with the reminder of an early morning departure for Grand Isle. After securing the main riggings, Jackson retired to his private bunk in the captain's quarters. While lighting his lantern, he heard something shift behind the wooden barrel in the corner.

"Sinbad, is that you back there?"

A calico cat meowed from the top bunk.

Instinctively, Jackson grabbed his sword and shoved the barrel aside with a swift kick. His sword swooped toward the scrunched-up figure in the corner then stopped abruptly at the sound of a gasp.

"What on earth...?" Jackson froze in place with the tip of his sword pointing at a startled young damsel.

"I'll thank you to put that sword away, sir."

"Excuse me?"

"I said, I'll thank you to put that sword away. You are in the presence of a lady. Where are your manners?"

Jackson stared back in disbelief. "Forgive me, Mademoiselle," he replied. "If I'm not mistaken, you are a stowaway on my ship."

Peyton rose slowly from her hunched position and straightened her gown with a brush of her hands. "I am not a stowaway. I am a guest."

"A guest?" Jackson laughed. "You, mademoiselle, are an *uninvited* guest who happens to be hiding in the captain's quarters of a ship full of men who would not be at all concerned with manners had any one of them found you instead of me."

The young woman lifted her chin, her eyes sparkling with defiance. "Sir, I am perfectly willing to pay a crossing fee if you'll be so kind as to give me a bed for the night— preferably in my own room. And, I am a bit famished. I'd appreciate a hot meal brought to my room once I get settled."

Jackson shook his head as though waking himself from an unreal dream. "Your own room? My entire crew all sleep in one room. The captain of the ship is the only one with his own quarters—which happens to be the cabin we are both occupying now. You must be under the false assumption that this is a luxury liner for passengers—which is about as far from the truth as you can get." He took a deep breath, amazed at the cheek of this interloper. "I hate to be rude, but trust me when I say that you are not at all safe among this crew of lonely seamen, so I am going to have to ask you to leave the same way you came."

"That's impossible. I came in a dinghy –which I'm afraid I sent afloat when I climbed aboard your ship."

Femme folle . "May I ask how you managed to climb board my ship from a dinghy?"

"It was quite a chore really, given that it was the dead of night, and climbing a rope ladder in a ball gown with a wet hem was no easy task either, then to sneak past your night watchman...."

Jackson bit back a curse. "I'll be speaking with my crew about that, but there is no way you are staying on this ship." He gave the young lady her marching orders in the same tone he used on his crew.

Peyton's bottom lip quivered. Then her shoulders fell and began to shake. She slid slowly back down the wall into her hunched position, dropped her face into her folded arms and sobbed.

If there was one thing Jackson had had little experience with, it was crying women. His life at sea had provided a safe haven from having to deal with the fairer sex. Until now. He had no idea what to say next. So, he said nothing, and just waited.

Her sobs grew louder.

"Aww, come on... what is it...why are you here anyway?"

"I'm r-running away," she sobbed.

"Running away from what?"

"From *him*. From marrying Lord Piggot."

"Lord Piggot?" Jackson stifled a laugh. "Is there really a man with such a name?"

"Exactly my point," Peyton replied. "How would you

like to have to marry some brutish old man and have your name changed to Peyton Piggot?"

Jackson paused to consider her plight. "I would find that extremely difficult," he stated. "So why do you have to marry him?"

"My stepfather made an arrangement with him. After my mother died, my stepfather lost our family fortune to gambling. He's counting on me to restore our family's future through this 'advantageous' marriage. Lord Piggot owns a sugar plantation—The Piggot Plantation—have you heard of it?"

"Can't say I have, but I don't spend much time on land." Jackson took a chair across from his stowaway and sighed heavily. "What's your name?"

"Peyton Abercrombie. And yours?"

"My real name is Jacques Lafitte."

"French?"

"Oui. My crew calls me Jackson because no one knows how to pronounce Jacques."

"Did you say your last name is Lafitte?" Peyton glanced around the room. "Oh my gosh; a sword, a crew of uncultured men, barrels and barrels of who knows what all…you, Jacques Lafitte, are a *pirate!*"

Jackson was impressed at her calculations. "What makes

you think that?"

"Everyone knows about Jean and Pierre Lafitte from France who pirated these waters for years. They're legends. Are you related?"

Jackson couldn't help but feel a twinge of pride that a pretty young lady was familiar with his family name. "It's rumored that I am, but I refrain from admitting anything that might be used against me."

"Wow. I'm on board a pirate ship!"

"I prefer to use the term cargo ship. Which brings me again to the point that women are rarely safe aboard such vessels."

"Oh, please let me stay—I promise I won't be any trouble. Where are you headed anyway?"

"Grand Isle, first light of day."

"I would love to go there." She clasped her hands together and smiled. "My mother's family has a summer cabin where I could stay once I get there. Please let me go just that far. I can stay hidden—no one will notice me. I'll be quiet as a mouse."

"No one will notice you in that bright green gown? Do you know how dangerous it is if my crew finds you on board?"

"Maybe I could borrow a pair of your trousers and dress

like a man. Just tell them you picked up a new crewmate."

"Besides the fact that I'm over a foot taller than you and twice as broad, there's no way that face of yours will pass for a man."

Peyton looked longingly into Jackson's eyes with a silent plea.

Jackson sighed. There was something about this vulnerable young woman soon to be thrust into the hands of a brutish man. Her pleas pulled at his heart in a manner he'd never experienced before. *I must be crazy to even consider such a request.* "I'll take you as far as Grand Isle—but that's it."

"Truly?" Peyton's adoring smile threatened to undo him.

"You're going to have stay hidden in here until we dock. I'm breaking my own rules to allow this." Jackson glanced around. "Where're you planning to sleep?"

Peyton glanced around the small cabin. "The top bunk looks fine to me."

"That's Sinbad's bed."

"Who's Sinbad?"

"My cat."

"Your cat? Pirates don't have cats, they have parrots. What kind of pirate are you, anyway?"

Peyton received a pair of raised eyebrows, strongly

suggesting that she was pushing her luck.

"Oh, fine, I'll sleep with your cat."

Read the rest here

Renee Riva is an ACFW award winning author who writes for WaterBrook/Random House, David C. Cook, and Winged Publications. Renee has been writing inspirational, humorous stories ever since she won her first writing contest in the second grade. She now enjoys writing clean romances for Forget Me Not Romances, a division of Winged Publications.

Renee's Booklist includes:

Saving Sailor Trilogy

Romances:

Happy Camper—a prequel to

Liza of Green Gables

Dawn's Gentle Light

Always Kiss Me Good Bye

Reluctant Cowgirl

A Chance of Rain

Jackson's Treasure

Sweetwater Café

Renee has a website: www.reneeriva.com and she can be contacted through thru this site.

Find them all on amazon.com or click here:

Renee's Bookshop

If you enjoyed this story, I would so appreciate an amazon review. Thank you so much!